# Chris Higgins

Illustrated by **Lee Wildish**

*Hodder
Children's
Books*

A division of Hachette Children's Books

Text copyright © 2012 Chris Higgins
Illustrations © 2012 Lee Wildish

First published in Great Britain in 2012
by Hodder Children's Books

The right of Chris Higgins and Lee Wildish to be identified as the
Author and Illustrator of the Work has been asserted by them in
accordance with the Copyright, Designs and Patents Act 1988

1

A Catalogue record for this book is available
from the British Library

ISBN  978 0 340 98984 5

Typeset and designed by Alyssa Peacock

Printed and bound in Great Britain by
Clays Ltd, St Ives plc

The paper and board used in this paperback by Hodder Children's Books
are natural recyclable products made from wood grown in sustainable
forests. The manufacturing processes conform to the environmental
regulations of the country of origin.

Hodder Children's Books
a division of Hachette Children's Books
338 Euston Road, London NW1 3BH
An Hachette UK company
www.hachette.co.uk

For *my* funny family

Thanks to Lucy for the title
and to Anne, Naomi and Ellen

# Chapter 1

At school we are doing seeds.

Dontie says *he* did seeds when he was in Miss Pocock's class and it's boring.

He's wrong.

It's not boring, it's **AMAZING**.

We watch a DVD in class.

It shows us how, if you plant a tiny little seed in a pot of dark, crumbly soil, before you know it, it will turn into a proper plant.

★ **MAGIC!** ★

The man on the DVD says that plants need light, air and water to grow.

Miss Pocock says, 'I wonder if he's telling the truth? Shall we do some experiments in science to find out!' and everyone shouts, 'Yeeesss!'

Some people in our class are growing mustard and cress on damp cotton wool on the window sill in the sunshine.

'That's easy-peasy,' says Lucinda.

Lucinda and I are doing something much harder.

We're trying to grow tomato plants in a pot. In the PE cupboard. In the dark.

Lucinda knows all about growing things because her mum has got a proper organic vegetable garden of her own.

'They won't like it in the dark,' she says as she presses her seed firmly down into the soil with her thumb.

I swallow hard, feeling sorry for the little tomato seeds.

'Imagine being pushed head first into the earth,' I say.

Lucinda snorts. 'I'd like to see someone try and push *me* head first into the earth.'

So would I. Lucinda can be very bossy sometimes.

I've got quite a lot of experience with bossy people. My sister, V, is bossy too.

'Your turn,' she says.

I place my tiny seed gently next to hers.

She scoops up heaps of soil and dumps it on top of them both.

Then she picks up the watering can and soaks them in cold water.

Then she puts them in the dark cupboard.

'They'll be all right,' she says, when

she sees my face. 'Worry Guts.'

All through literacy I can't concentrate.

I keep thinking about the poor little seeds buried alive in the darkness, freezing cold and wet through.

Trapped underground like those people in the earthquake, on the news.

I had nightmares about those people for weeks.

Now I'll have nightmares about the seeds.

# Chapter 2

I get **THREE** questions wrong in literacy.
I get **FOUR** spellings wrong in the test.
I get **FIVE** sums wrong in numeracy.
In tower ball I stop counting how many times I drop the ball.
After **TEN**.

I'm always like this when I'm worried. Mum says my brain changes to spaghetti

and gets all tangled up and I think she must be right because I can't think straight.

Every single day of my life there is something to worry about.

I need to talk to Miss Pocock. Alone.

At the end of school I take ages packing my bag but there are still people left in the classroom. So I go to my peg and sit down and wait.

Finally everyone is gone. Except for Miss Pocock who is at her table marking a big pile of books.

'Yes, Mattie?' she asks without looking up.

I don't know how she knows I'm still there in the classroom. Dontie said she had eyes in the back of her head when he was in her classroom.

I think she's got them on the top of her head as well.

'What's the matter today?' she says, putting down her pen and looking at me.

'They won't like it,' I blurt out.

'What?'

'The tomato seeds.'

'Come again?'

She takes her glasses off and rubs her proper eyes. They're kind but tired-looking.

'We watered them loads. They'll be freezing to death in that dark old cupboard.'

'It's an experiment, Mattie. To see if they can grow without light.'

'But they'll die if we don't rescue them!'

Miss Pocock sighs.

'Yes, you're probably right.' She unlocks the PE cupboard. 'Look, we'll stand them in the sun, shall we? They'll soon warm up.'

I feel better then.

But a few days later the cotton wool has sprouted little cottontails of mustard and cress that wave about in the air and our pot is just full of earth. I poke about in it to look for tails but there are none to be seen.

'Leave it alone!' orders Lucinda. 'You'll kill them!'

I snatch my hand away but it's too late. Lucinda and I check them again at lunchtime. Nothing.

'What's up, Mattie?' asks Miss Pocock who is eating her yoghurt at her table.

I gaze at her in sorrow. 'The seeds are dead. I've killed them.'

'They're not dead. They're just not

ready yet,' explains Miss Pocock. 'They need to germinate.'

'See! I told you,' Lucinda says, which is a lie.

Germination doesn't mean you've got germs; it means you've taken root and developed. Miss Pocock explains it to us in the afternoon then makes the whole class write it up and draw a diagram for homework.

Lucinda says it's my fault the class has got homework but for once I don't care.

Because this morning, when I get to school, Miss Pocock says, 'Look Mattie, your seeds are starting to sprout,' and there are two tiny green shoots poking up through the soil.

They've germinated.

# Chapter 3

I can't wait to tell Mum. But she's late today.

Dontie doesn't mind; he's playing keepy-uppy with his football in the school yard.

V gets cross.

V is my younger sister, aged 7. Dontie is my older brother. He's 11 and will be going to the big school in September. I'm 9 and I'm called Mattie. My real name is Matisse, after the painter.

Dontie is named after a painter too. His real name is Donatello.

That's because my Dad's an artist.

But V is named after Aunty Etna's favourite singer,
Vera Lynn.

Mum said she'd had enough of artists by the time V was born. V hates her name so we just call her V for short.

The other members of our family are Stanika, Jellico, Uncle Vesuvius and Grandma and Granddad.

We are the Butterfields.

Stanika are actually two people, Stanley who is 4 and Anika who is 2. Anika was born on Stanley's second birthday.

'She's your birthday present, Stan,' said Mum and placed her, wrapped up in a blanket, in his arms. 'You've got to be a big boy now and look after your little sister. Can you do that for me?'

He nodded, his face serious. Stan is a man of his word. Ever since then he's lugged Anika around with him everywhere he goes. They're always together so everyone calls them Stanika.

Actually, Stan is not a big boy at all and Anika has grown a lot. She's huge. Every time he sits down Anika sits on his lap and he disappears because she's big and round and squashy and he's small and thin and wiry.

But she can't speak yet.

'Doesn't need to,' shrugs Mum when Grandma tells her to get Anika checked out. 'Stan says everything for her.'

Grandma's always telling Mum what to do.

Mum doesn't always listen though.

We're the only children left in the playground.

'Where's Mum?' whines V. She hates school and can't wait to get home.

'She won't be long,' Dontie says

automatically, but it's too late, I've started to worry.

Maybe Stanika have got lost or the house has burned down or a robber has broken in and tied them all up or...

'Here she is,' says Dontie, tucking his football under his arm.

Mum is hurrying up the street towards us, pushing Anika in the buggy with Stan running along beside her, holding on tight. Jellico is on the lead which is looped over the handle and tangled round his legs so he's doing a sort of hop, skip and jump.

'Where've you been?' complains V. 'We've been waiting for ages.'

'Sorry kids,' pants Mum, red-cheeked and out of breath. 'I got held up at the doctor's.'

Alarm bells jangle inside my head.

'I'm starving!' moans V.

'Me too,' says Dontie.

'What for?'

'What?' says Mum.

'What were you at the doctor's for?'
I repeat.

Mum gives me one of her now-don't-you-start looks.

'Nothing for you to worry about,'
she says firmly.

All right for her to say.

# Chapter 4

On the way home we call in at Kumars to buy stuff for tea. V picks up a tube of Smarties.

'Put those back,' says Mum without even looking up.

I think she's got eyes in the top of her head too because it's bent over a large packet of fish fingers.

She's checking the price.

She sniffs and puts them in the wire basket.

'Can I have crisps then?'

'No.'

'It's not fair!' grumbles V. 'I'm starving to death.'

Even I know this is extremely unlikely. V's always eating. Mum says she doesn't know where she puts it all because she's thin and wiry like a coat hanger, not a bit like me.

Granddad calls her a SKINNY WHIPPET.

Grandma calls me **well-padded**.

'Can we have chips for tea then?' asks V, changing tack.

'All right.' Mum bends over the freezer and pulls out a bag of oven chips and a packet of frozen peas.

'Anika doesn't like peas,' says Stanley.

Actually, this is not true.

*Stanley* doesn't like peas.

Sometimes he makes things up about Anika to suit himself.

Mum picks up an apple pie, looks at the price and puts it back.

'Anika loves apple pie,' says Stan, longingly.

Mum sighs and picks it up again and puts it in her basket.

'My seeds have germinated,' I remember.

'Bingo!' she says. 'You must have green fingers.'

I study my hands, puzzled.

'That means you're good at growing things.'

An idea pops out of my brain.

'We could grow our own apples,' I say. 'For apple pie.'

'What? In time for tea?' says Mum.

'We could grow all our own fruit.

And vegetables.'

'Steady on,' says Mum.

'It's easy. We could grow tomatoes... and cucumber...' I look around for inspiration and spot some jam on the shelves. 'And raspberries and strawberries...'

'Strawberries!' breathes Stan. 'Anika loves strawberries.'

'Can we grow our own chips?' asks V.

'We could grow our own potatoes and make chips,' says Mum.

'Can we?' I ask, my stomach spinning in excitement.

'No, I didn't mean that...'

'£7.21 please,' says Mr Kumar.

'Oh flip,' says Mum. She rummages in her purse and pulls a face. 'Not enough. We'd better put this back.' She hands the apple pie to Dontie who drops it into the freezer.

Mr Kumar glowers at him.

Stanika gaze at Mum sorrowfully.

V opens her mouth to object.

'Home!' says Mum briskly and V closes it again.

I don't think Mum's got as much money as she would like.

And she's been to the doctor's.

That's two new things for me to worry about.

# Chapter 5

At home Mum tells V to sit down and practise her reading while she listens. V says, 'It's not fair!' lots of times but Mum makes her do it anyway. V hates reading. Dontie disappears onto the computer and I wander outside followed by Stanika and Jellico.

'What are we doing?' asks Stanley.

'Looking for a vegetable patch.'

We look in the front garden first. It doesn't take long. It's concreted over so our car can sit on it when we're not using it.

Except for weeds growing through the cracks there's nothing else growing there at all.

'Round the back,' I say.

We troop around in single file, squeezing through the gap in the broken fence. Anika gets stuck but Stan manages to push her through. She's well-padded like me but more smiley.

Our back garden is far more interesting. It's long and narrow and stretches all the way down to the railway. It's full of overgrown trees and bushes and long grass. Hidden amongst them are rusty old bikes and abandoned toys, bleached by the sun.

There's lots going on in our garden.

In the summer brilliant red poppies leap up to surprise you.

Tall nettles appear and sting your legs and fat dock leaves appear to make them better.

A twisty, mean old plant with big white flowers like trumpets snakes itself around all the other plants and squeezes them so tightly they can't breathe. Dontie grabs the end of it and pulls it out of the ground but it always comes back.

By the back door there's an old wooden bench that has lost some of its slats and a washing line that spins around. Dontie uses it for pull-ups and V hangs upside down from it, showing her knickers.

But best of all, it's full of Dad's sculptures.

**MY DAD** is soooo clever.

**MY DAD** is tall and thin with a soft tickly beard that goes right round his chin from one ear to the other.

**MY DAD** works in the local college teaching art, but as well as being a painter, he's a sculptor too.

MY DAD was going to be an engineer and make lots of money but then he met Mum on holiday.

So MY DAD left university and married her and became an artist instead.

And he became MY DAD.

One day Lucinda said to me, 'Sometimes I get sick of hearing about Your Dad,' which I thought was a bit mean. Lucinda never talks about her dad any more.

Mum says Grandma's never forgiven her for leading Dad astray.

I think she's right. Once I heard Grandma say to Granddad, 'Our Tim would have gone places if he hadn't had his head turned by Mona.'

It sounded like Dad's head was facing one way but then it spotted Mum and swivelled round in another direction.

I'm not surprised Dad's head turned. Mum is really pretty, everyone notices her. Dad calls her his Mona Lisa after the painting.

Lucinda says she looks too young to be our mum, she looks like a teenager. I think *her* mum looks like a grandma, but I didn't tell her that.

Mum is skinny like V and she wears vest tops and tight jeans and shoes which Grandma says are, 'Much too high, you'll have bunions if you're not careful.'

I wasn't too sure what bunions were, they sounded like a mixture of buns and onions. So I asked Lucinda because she knows everything.

She screwed up her face and said, 'YUCK! My nan's got those, they're disgusting! They're great big lumps on

26

the side of your feet that make your toes turn in like this, look!' and she pushed her big toe over her other toes as far as it could go.

I got worried then that Mum's toes would turn in too but I watched them every day for a month and they didn't move at all.

I think Grandma's wrong for once. I can't ever imagine Mum with bunions and twisted toes because she's got tiny, pretty feet and she paints her toenails red.

Mum scrapes her long blonde hair up high in a pony tail too and wears dangly earrings that Anika loves playing with and jangly bracelets and she would never, ever leave the house without her black eyeliner on and a bit of lippy.

'We girls have got to keep up appearances, haven't we Mattie?' she says and spritzes us both with the scent Dad bought her for Christmas which was dead expensive and is just about the best thing you have ever smelt in your whole life.

I love my mum.

I wonder why she went to the doctor's?

# Chapter 6

I don't like to boast but Dad's sculptures are brilliant. He makes all sorts of things out of stone: people, animals, birds, insects, fish and fantastic mythical creatures.

He makes us one each for our birthdays, including our very first proper birthday, the day we were born. As soon as we're old enough to choose, we get to pick what we want. Stan chooses for Anika.

So far, in our back garden, we've got:

5 dinosaurs

2 fairies

an owl

an angel

a helicopter

Batman

2 kangaroos
boxing each other
(Stanika's 4th and
2nd birthdays)

a dragon

a racing car

a cat, a dog
and a goat

a penguin

a dalek

a gnome which looks
like Uncle Vesuvius

an eagle

2 loggerhead turtles
(Stanika's 3rd and
1st birthdays)

Superman

a praying mantis

a ghost

3 dolphins

a hedgehog

a spaceship

2 cherubs
(Stanika's 2nd and
very-first-as-in-
proper-day-Anika-
was-born birthdays)

a tractor

a shark

a digger truck

and a polar bear.

Between us, counting Dontie's, mine and V's proper-days-we-were-born birthdays, we are 38 sculptures old.

There's not a lot of space left.

'I wish my dad would make me a hedgehog from a block of stone,' sighed Lucinda when she saw my last birthday present.

'I didn't make it, it was already there,' explained Dad. 'I just teased it out with my chisel.'

Poor Lucinda. Her dad is an accountant and he spends all day making money.

But now he's lost his job.

Lucinda told me the other day her parents don't seem to like each other much any more because they're always arguing.

I hope my mum and dad never stop liking each other.

Stanley pushes Anika up onto the polar bear and gets up behind her.

'Giddy-up!' he calls and slaps the bear. Anika squeals with delight and bounces up and down and Stanley has to grab her tight around the middle to stop her sliding off. Jellico jumps up, barking encouragement, his tail wagging furiously.

Jellico is our big, scruffy dog who bounds about all over the place. His hair gets everywhere. Mum says one day she'll knit Stanley a jumper with it but he's still waiting. Dontie's supposed to brush him every day but he forgets.

I don't think Jellico minds. He's named after a painter too, Fra Angelico, but that's a bit of a mouthful so we just call him Jellico. Mum thinks he's got some sheepdog in him because he spends his time rounding us all up and barking at the postman.

I poke about a bit with a stick, trying to find a piece of ground large enough to grow vegetables in. Jellico drops down to help me, sniffing at the earth.

'What are you up to?' says a voice.

# Chapter 7

Uncle Vesuvius is peering over the fence.

He must be standing on something because he's not very tall, though he's very old. He's wearing a vest, and braces to keep his trousers up, and Aunty Etna's straw hat to keep the sun off his head. It's a bit battered now. The hat, I mean, not his head. Though, actually, that's a bit battered too. He's got a biro hanging from his mouth.

'I'm looking for a vegetable plot.'

'What for?'

Sometimes Uncle Vez can be a bit slow on the uptake. That's all right. Mum says I'm very patient.

'To grow vegetables in.'

'Good idea.'

'Then Mum won't have to buy them from the shop.'

'Very sensible.'

'But I can't find one.'

He takes the biro out of his mouth between his fingers and breathes out pretend smoke. He stopped smoking cigarettes when Aunty Etna got ill.

Uncle Vesuvius is Aunty Etna's husband. I don't think those are their real names.

Mum called them that because they both smoked a lot when she was growing up and Uncle Vesuvius belched quite a bit too. They were Mum's foster parents. Mum says they were like two volcanoes waiting to go off.

But now Aunty Etna's dead and Uncle Vesuvius has given up smoking. He still belches though. Aunty Etna gave up too but it was too late for her. Now Uncle Vez smokes biros instead.

'I can clear a bit o' ground for you if you want.' He taps pretend ash from the biro onto the grass.

'Yes please!'

'Right then, I'll get me spade.'

Uncle Vez puts his biro back between his lips and disappears. Jellico and I sit down to wait while Stanika explore the arctic regions of our garden on their friendly polar bear. Soon Uncle Vez returns. I can hear him talking to Mum inside the house.

Before long he comes out into the back garden, carrying his spade and a rake. We watch as he sets to, raking and bending, digging and clearing, stopping occasionally to groan a bit and puff on his biro.

Mum comes to the back step.

'Tea's ready.'

A voice calls from inside the house.

'Anyone at home?'

Mum's eyes close. 'Perfect timing,' she says. But I don't think she means it.

It's Grandma and Granddad.

# Chapter 8

Grandma is Dad's mother and Granddad is Dad's father. Grandma likes to tell Mum what to do. It's funny that Grandma knows more about bringing up children than Mum because she only had one child, Dad, and Mum's got five, us.

'Anika doesn't like peas,' Stanley reminds Mum at teatime with a frown. '*And* she's still hungry.'

Anika's peas are all gone but Stanley's are still there, arranged neatly at the side of his plate.

'I'll eat them!' says V and spoons them into her mouth before Grandma has time to object.

'Oh dear, I forgot,' says Mum. 'I'd better do her some baked beans instead. Would you like some too, Stanley?'

Stanley's face clears. 'Yes please,' he nods. Anika's head nods too.

Grandma snorts. 'You spoil those children.'

Stanley's face falls. So does Anika's.

Sometimes Grandma talks about us as if she doesn't like us very much. Like when she says, '*Those* children.'

Mum says nothing. She opens the cupboard and takes out a tin of beans.

'I don't like peas either,' says V loyally. 'Even though I ate them up.'

'You children are too fussy by half,' says Grandma. 'You should eat what you're given and be grateful.'

V scowls. Grandma gets Anika out of her highchair and sits her on her knee for a cuddle. But Anika wants to sit on Stanley. She wriggles about and knocks over the open bottle of tomato ketchup which spills out over the table.

'Anika!' snaps Grandma and Anika, startled, howls and reaches for Stanley. Stanley jumps up to get her and knocks over his juice.

'Mona!' shrieks Grandma. 'See what these children of yours are up to!'

Mum turns round looking harassed. 'Don't worry, Mum,' says Dontie, dabbing his chips in the puddle of ketchup decorating the table. 'I'll eat it up.'

'Stop that!' barks Grandma, and raps him on the knuckles with a spoon. 'Where are your manners?'

'Ouch!' says Dontie and glares at Grandma.

The puddle drips off the table onto the floor. Jellico licks it up.

Grandma and Granddad always come at teatime.

I don't mean to be horrible but sometimes I wish they didn't.

'It's the only time we get to see you all together,' says Grandma.

But it's the very worst time to see us all together because:

🐌 By teatime, Anika's grouchy and wants to go to bed. Grandma wants to cuddle her but Anika only wants Stanley.

🐌 Stanley gets nervous with Grandma around.

🐌 V's always in a bad mood because Mum makes her practise her reading before tea and she can't do it.

🐌 Dontie's grumpy because he knows Grandma will tell him off. Lots.

🐌 Mum is stressed because she wants to get us into bed and Grandma wants to get us to behave.

🐌 Dad's not home yet anyway and that's who Grandma really wants to see.

🐌 I'm probably at my most worried at this time of day.

Now I have Four Worry Questions in my head turning my brain to spaghetti.

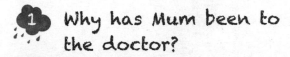 Why has Mum been to the doctor?

How will we eat if Mum doesn't have enough money to feed us?

What if Mum and Dad stop liking each other?

Why doesn't Grandma like us sometimes?

# Chapter 9

I only have time to whisper the last question to Mum quickly in the kitchen. Mum says, 'Oh, Mattie!' and gives me a big hug. 'Grandma likes us all very, very much indeed but she has got STANDARDS.'

I don't think Granddad has got standards because he's a lot quieter than she is and doesn't complain about us. He's a bit like Dad, tall and thin, only he's got grey hair and a grey moustache instead of black hair and a black beard, and he's retired.

I'm not sure what he did when he worked but it must have been something important because Mum says he deserves a flipping medal.

When Dad comes home everyone cheers up, including Grandma.

Especially Grandma.

Her face shines like someone's switched a light on inside her head.

Dad throws his bag on the floor and swings Anika up to the ceiling 'til she squeals with delight, then he does the same to Stanley, then to V who pretends not to like it but she does really. He's a bit puffed out by then so he just ruffles my hair and pretends to box with Dontie, then he disappears into the kitchen to see Mum.

When they come out Mum's lost her harassed look and is looking pink and pretty again.

'What's he doing?' Dad looks out of the window at Uncle Vesuvius who's spreading something dark on the garden.

'Making a vegetable plot,' I explain. A nice patch of earth has appeared between the fairies and the dinosaurs.

'Great idea!' says Dad. 'I'll go and give him a hand.'

'Come and have a look at our vegetable plot, everybody!' yells V and opens the back door. A strange smell, rich and sour, invades the house. Everyone looks at Anika. It smells like her nappies only worse.

'What's that stink?' V screws up her

nose in disgust.

Uncle Vesuvius bends down and crumbles the soil between his fingers.

'Needed some dressing,' he declares.

'What kind of dressing?' asks V.

'Salad dressing,' says Dontie.

'Window dressing,' says Mum.

'Dressing up,' says Dad.

'Dressing down,' says Mum.

'Dressing tables,' says Dontie.

'Dressing gowns,' says Mum.

'Un-dressing,' says Dontie.

'Ad-dressing,' says Mum.

'Stop it!' yells V, her hands on her ears.

Uncle Vez lifts up his hat and scratches his head, studying the three of them as if they're daft.

'Manure,' he says.

'What's manure?' asks V.

'Horse muck,' he replies. He leans on his spade and blows a pretend smoke ring with his biro, looking pleased with himself. 'Found it on the road.'

Uncle Vesuvius has plastered our

vegetable plot with horse muck.

'Horse poo!' screeches V. 'I'm not eating vegetables grown in horse poo.'

She's got a point.

Even Grandma looks surprised.

At least she doesn't say, 'You'll eat what you're given and be grateful,' which is what she normally says.

# Chapter 10

Mum can't put her washing out for a few days, but then Uncle Vesuvius rakes it over again and the problem of the stinky vegetable plot disappears. Soon V forgets all about the horse poo and it's time to sow some seeds.

'Where are they?' she asks. I think she's quite excited by all this.

'What?'

'Duh! The seeds?'

V can be very annoying when she starts

off her sentences with 'Duh!'

'Where do we get them from?' she persists.

I try to remember what Miss Pocock taught us.

'You get them from plants.'

'But we haven't got any plants,' points out V.

A niggle of worry starts writhing around in my tummy. 'Dontie?'

Dontie yawns. 'Ask Uncle Vez.'

It's OK. Uncle Vesuvius says I'm quite right, normally you would get seeds from plants. That's the best way. But as we're starting off it's all right to buy them for the first time.

'From a seed shop?' asks V.

'From a catalogue,' says Uncle Vez.

'I knew that,' says V, but she didn't.

Sometimes Mum uses the catalogue to buy our clothes from. I didn't know it sold seeds too.

A few days later Uncle Vez brings a catalogue in for us to look at. It's a special gardening magazine full of luscious fruit and brightly coloured vegetables.

'You choose,' he says. 'Two each.'

'Me first!' bags V. She picks big, round, red strawberries and delicious-looking raspberries but Uncle Vez says it's too late for fruit and we'll be better off with veg if we're growing from seed.

So V throws a strop and says it's stupid and she's not going to do it after all.

'Suit yourself,' says Uncle Vez.

Dontie goes next. He chooses lettuce because Uncle Vez says it's easy to grow and rocket because he likes the sound of it and it's even easier.

Stanika choose carrots and beetroot and sweetcorn and peas, because they like the colours.

'You don't like peas,' Mum reminds Stanley.

'Anika does,' he says, smiling bravely.

I choose beans because there's a picture of them growing and they have pretty flowers on them, and squash because it sounds funny.

'Can you grow squash?' asks V, who can't help ear-wigging even though she thinks it's stupid.

'Yeah.' Dontie looks up with a grin.

'How does it grow?'

'In bottles,' says Dontie. 'You get orange squash trees and lemon squash trees.'

V looks from Dontie to Mum, sensing

a trap. Mum shakes her head slightly.

'No you don't,' V says uncertainly. 'Do you, Mum?'

'It's not that sort of squash, pet,' says Mum, trying not to laugh. 'It's like pumpkin.'

'I knew that,' says V quickly, which is something she says quite often. She's interested again now. She chooses pumpkin because she wants one for Halloween ('Should be just ready by then,' agrees Uncle Vez.) and spinach because Dad says someone called Popeye eats it and he's super-strong.

Mum chooses sprouts which will be ready in time for Christmas dinner and everyone groans.

Then a week later the postman brings them all in a big brown box.

# Chapter 11

The first nice day we have, we plant

 spinach 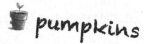 pumpkins

 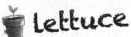 squash

 beans  rocket

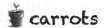 lettuce  peas

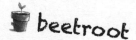 carrots 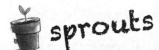 sprouts

beetroot

and sweetcorn

in rows, straight into the ground. Grandma and Granddad come around to give us a hand.

'You should start them off in a greenhouse first,' says Grandma, taking charge as usual.

'We haven't got one,' says Mum flatly.

'Ground's warm enough,' says Uncle Vez. 'S'all they want, bit of sun, bit of earth, bit of rain,' and much to my surprise, Grandma agrees.

'What happens if it doesn't rain?' I say anxiously, looking up at the cloudless sky.

'You water 'em,' says Uncle Vez and plonks a watering can in front of us.

'Me first!' says V and one by one she squashes her pumpkin seeds flat into the soil and scatters loose earth on top of them. She reminds me of Lucinda. She dusts the earth from her palms and stands up, looking very pleased with herself, then does a little skip around the garden.

When she gets back Stanika are on their knees carefully planting their carrot seeds, their tongues caught between their teeth in identical concentration. V lets out a wail of anguish which makes us all jump.

'What's the matter?' says Mum.

'They're planting their seeds on top of mine!'

'No, they're not, banana head, yours are here,' says Dontie.

'Where?' V looks around wildly. 'I can't see them any more! I don't know where I put them!'

'Here!' He digs at the earth with the toe of his shoe, exposing an oval-shaped pumpkin seed like a mini rugby ball.

'But I'll never remember where they are!' she cries, working herself up into a paddy. 'Then I won't be able to water them and they'll shrivel up underground and die!'

My heart sinks. She's right. It was easy to look after the tomato seeds at school because they were in pots. But this is different.

Once we'd planted our seeds in the ground we'd never find them again. One patch of earth looks much the same as another.

Grandma catches my eye. 'Hold on a minute!' she says and disappears into the house. When she comes back she's carrying her knitting bag with her. She delves into it and brings out a small ball

of bright red wool that she's got left over
from V's Christmas jumper.

She picks up a bit of stick, ties the end
of the wool around it, bends over and
pokes it into the ground. Then she unfurls
it along the row of pumpkin seeds and
fastens it to a stick at the other end.

'Now you'll remember where your seeds
are,' she says.

V's face breaks into a smile.

'What colour was your Christmas jumper, Stanley?' asks Grandma and Stanley thinks for a minute and says 'Blue,' so Grandma digs around in her bag 'til she finds a piece of blue wool.

'And we all know what yours is, Anika,' she says and we all yell 'Pink!' because Anika is wearing it. My little sister beams with pleasure and takes the piece of pink wool from Grandma in her plump little fist.

Grandma gives me some green wool and Dontie some purple and then we all go hunting for sticks to tie our wool on to, so we can remember where our seeds are when we've planted them.

And when we've finished our vegetable plot looks beautiful with bright strands of red and blue and pink and green and purple wool fluttering in the breeze to remind us of the tiny seeds busily germinating away beneath the ground.

Good old Grandma.

# Chapter 12

Seeds take ages to germinate. About 10 days.

I know this already from the school tomato plants, but V and Stanika don't and they are so impatient, especially V. She keeps checking hers every five minutes.

'A watched pot never boils,' says Uncle Vez as he sits down at the table for his tea with us.

Actually, this is not true because Mum asked me to watch the rice so it didn't boil dry and I never took my eyes off the pot once, not even for a second, and it was boiling all the time.

'They'll come when they're ready,' he says. He's here for tea because Mum's made corned beef curry, his favourite. 'We used to eat this during the war,' he tells us, which is what he says every single time he has it.

He eats very fast and noisily, bending low over his food, slurping it up and smacking his lips with satisfaction.

Stanley copies him so Anika does too.

'No waste then, we were all on rations!' sniffs Grandma.

She and Granddad appeared as usual just as we sat down for our tea and Mum's face fell. Granddad's reading the paper and Grandma's joined us at the table even though she doesn't want anything to eat.

'Were you in the war, Grandma?' asks Dontie with interest.

'No! How old do you think I am?' replies Grandma indignantly. I think it's one of those questions that are not meant to be answered because when V opens her mouth to hazard a guess, Mum gives her one of her warning looks and she closes it again.

'I was a dear little baby just like you when the war was on,' Grandma says, leaning across to Anika in her high chair and tickling her little fat feet. Anika laughs and spoons more curry into her smiley mouth, bending low over her bowl just like Uncle Vez.

But then Grandma says sharply, 'Mind

your manners, Anika! Sit up and eat nicely. And stop slurping, Stanley!'

Stanley drops his fork on the floor in surprise and Anika's mouth falls open and curry dribbles down her chin. Grandma tuts and picks up the fork and goes to wash it under the tap. Then she scrubs Anika's face clean with a wet flannel.

'Aren't you eating anything, Mona?' she says, sitting back down again. She pushes Anika's spoon at her but Anika curls her hand into a fist and turns her head away. Grandma frowns.

'Naughty girl!' she says.

'She doesn't want it,' says Stanley quietly.

'When I want your opinion I'll ask for it!' says Grandma and tries to spoon more food into Anika's mouth. Anika's mouth clamps shut and she stares at

Mum glumly with big, sad eyes.

'I think she's had enough,' says Mum.

'I've had enough too,' says Stanley and puts his fork down.

Grandma glares at him. 'There's too much waste in this family!'

V takes one longing look at the rest of her curry then puts her fork down too. She scowls at Grandma. Grandma scowls back.

They look like a mirror image of each other.

Now I know what V will look like in 60 years time.

# Chapter 13

Nobody seems to feel like eating any more, except for Uncle Vez. We sit there in silence until he's hoovered his plate clean and sat back with a satisfied belch.

'Pardon me!' he says. 'Very nice, our Mona.'

Grandma looks at the rest of our plates which are still half-full and announces to no one in particular, 'Good food costs money you know! Money doesn't grow on trees!'

'Wish it did. I'd plant money seeds in the vegetable plot,' says Uncle Vez and Dontie laughs.

But Mum's not laughing. She gets up and collects the plates without a word. Grandma gets up too.

'Sit down, Mona. I'll do those. You finish your meal.'

'No,' says Mum. 'I'm not very hungry.'

Grandma's mouth sets in a straight line of disapproval. Then she says, 'How can you expect your children to eat up their meals if you don't?'

Mum doesn't answer.

'You'll make yourself ill if you don't eat,' persists Grandma.

'I'm fine,' says Mum quietly.

'You're looking thin, Mona. Peaky. You need to keep your energy up to look after this lot properly.'

I don't like it when Grandma calls us all 'this lot'. It makes us sound like Mum's got too many children and she should sort us out and send the ones she doesn't want any more off to the jumble sale in big black bin-bags.

'I DO look after them properly!' says Mum so loudly it makes Stanika and me jump. Her face has gone pink.

Granddad shuffles his paper and clears his throat. 'Of course you do, love,' he says. 'They're a credit to you. Aren't they Marjorie?'

Grandma doesn't answer and everything goes quiet and still.

Uncle Vez leans back in his chair with his hands behind his head and examines the ceiling.

Dontie puts his hands in his pockets and studies the wall.

V glares at Grandma.

Stanika stare at each other, round-eyed.

Jellico whines and shuffles under the table on his tummy.

I suck in my breath and start counting

in my head. One and 2 and 3 and 4...

Grandma looks at Granddad and he nods gently and she looks like V again when she's about to cry. I get to 'and 10' and think I'm going to burst, then Grandma says, 'Of course they are,' in a soft, trembly voice and suddenly I can breathe again.

'I didn't mean...' Her voice breaks off then she adds, 'I'm just concerned about you Mona, that's all. You seem a bit off colour.'

'I'm fine!' repeats Mum and stops gripping the draining board and starts to wash up. Grandma gets up from the table and stands next to her, a tea towel at the ready, but Mum says, 'It's all right, I can manage,' and her voice doesn't sound like hers, it sounds snappy.

Grandma sits back down again without another word.

Not long after, Grandma and Granddad leave, even though Dad's not home yet.

# Chapter 14

I'm in bed. Next to me V, curled up in a ball, is dead to the world, her knees jabbed sharply into the hollow of my back.

From the next room I can hear Stanika making soft snuffly noises. From the back bedroom comes the sound of Dontie snoring.

All the Butterfield children are asleep except for me.

Grandma's words keep tearing round my head like one of those annoying songs that gets on your nerves but you can't stop singing it. I can't switch them off.

I try locking them up behind the Worry Door like Mum told me to do if ever I'm worried about something. But it springs back open and the words spill out.

Now they're zooming round and round my spaghetti brain, screaming out loud and overtaking each other, like a Formula One race on the telly.

You're looking thin, Mona ... peaky ...
you seem a bit off colour ...
You'll make yourself ill, Mona
you're looking thin ... peaky ...
You'll make yourself ill ...

Aunty Etna was ill. Seriously ill.

First she went thin and peaky.

Then she went a funny colour.

And then…

I whimper and fling myself face down on my pillow, pulling the duvet over my head. V turns over, grumbling in her sleep, and snatches the duvet back.

Downstairs I can just make out the quiet murmur of voices. Mum's and Dad's.

Quiet as a mouse so I don't disturb V, I slip out of bed and tiptoe downstairs.

The living room door is shut tight but I can hear Mum and Dad talking inside.

My dad's got a big, loud voice and normally when you're in bed at night you can hear him laughing and sometimes even though he's downstairs, you can make out what he's saying.

But tonight I can't, even though he's only the other side of the wall. His voice is too low.

I sit down on the bottom step of the stairs in my nightie and pick at the scab on my knee.

In Lucinda's house the bottom step is the naughty step.

We don't have a naughty step. If we did V would spend all day on it said Mum, and what would be the point of that?

I love my mum.

My scab comes off. Underneath the skin is pink and shiny like the bottom of Anika's feet when Mum lifts her out of the bath.

A tiny spot of blood appears.

I bend my head and lick it off. It tastes sour.

Another spot takes its place and I squeeze it and it wells up and trickles down my leg.

I start crying.

The door opens and Dad's head appears.

'What are you doing there?' asks Dad.

I sob louder.

Mum's head appears beneath his.

'What's up, Mattie?' She spots my knee. 'Have you hurt yourself?'

'Noooooo!' I moan.

Dad bends down and picks me up. He staggers a bit but he doesn't put me down. Instead he says, 'Come on big girl, let's have a cuddle.'

We go into the living room and shut the door.

## Chapter 15

I am sitting on the sofa between my parents, having a cuddle sandwich. Jellico is lying by my feet with his head on his paws, winking at me.

When I mentioned to Lucinda once how in our house we have cuddle sandwiches, she wrinkled up her nose and said, 'What's a cuddle sandwich?'

I stared at her in surprise. 'You know! When you're in the middle and two people give you a cuddle at once, one on each side.'

'Oh yeah,' she said. 'We have those too.' But her face looked a bit blank.

I don't think she was telling the truth.

I don't think two people give her a cuddle at the same time any more. Not since her parents stopped liking each other.

Remembering this makes me cry a bit more.

'What's up, Mattie?' asks Mum, smoothing my hair away from my wet cheek.

'Stop crying,' says Dad, mopping my eyes with his hanky, 'and tell us what's wrong.'

I grab the hanky and blow my nose loudly in it. Then I try to get the Things I'm Worried About list straight in my head but my spaghetti brain has scrambled it all up.

At last I take a deep breath and decide to say the **REALLY BIG WORRY** that's bothering me most of all.

But I don't want to say it out loud in case it makes it happen so it comes out quiet and squeaky and Mum and Dad have to bend their heads to hear it.

'Mum's all thin and peaky...'

'No I'm not,' says Mum, looking indignant.

'And she's going to make herself ill if she doesn't eat...'

'No she won't,' says Dad looking puzzled.

Mum's eyes open wide. 'Oh, I get it! I know where this is coming from,' she says.

'And then she'll DIE LIKE AUNTY ETNA!!!'

My quiet, squeaky voice suddenly explodes into an enormous howl. Mum and Dad jump back in surprise and Jellico howls too.

'This is all your flipping mother's fault!' Mum says to Dad, sounding really cross. 'Shut up, Jellico!'

'Don't be angry with Dad!' I wail. 'I don't want you to get divorced!'

'Divorce?' says Dad bemused. 'Who's getting divorced?'

'Lucinda's parents. They don't like each other any more.'

'Really?' says Mum in her interested voice then she adds quickly, 'I'm sure that's not true!'

'They might,' I sob. 'Some people do.'

'Well we're not!' says Mum. 'We like each other.'

'A lot,' agrees Dad.

They are both smiling crinkly-eyed at each other.

'Shall we?' asks Dad.

'Shall we what?' asks Mum.

'Tell her,' says Dad.

I stop crying.

'Tell me what?'

# Chapter 16

Mum's having another baby!

'When?' I ask. I'm so excited. There are only three people in the whole wide world who know this fact. Mum, Dad and me.

'Not for a while. Not 'til around Christmas.'

'Christmas!'

'Yes. The baby's got to grow a bit in my tummy before it's ready to be born.'

'Like Anika did.' My brain pings. 'Is that why you went to the doctor's?'

'Yes.'

'So you're not ill and peaky?'

'No,' Mum laughs. 'Just pregnant and peaky. But soon I'll be pregnant and fat.'

'I like you fat.' I glow with happiness. 'Can I tell Lucinda?'

'No,' says Mum hastily. 'Let's just keep it to ourselves for a bit, shall we? Just you, me and Dad.'

'And the doctor,' I remind her.

'And the doctor,' she repeats. 'But we won't tell anyone else.'

'Not Dontie?'

'No.'

'Not V?'

'No.'

'Not Grandma?'

Mum makes a funny little noise in her throat, sort of half-gasp, half-giggle. 'No.

Especially not Grandma. Not just yet. It will be our little secret for the time being.'

'OK.' I hug the secret to myself like a soft, squashy cushion. We're going to have a new person in our family and apart from Mum, Dad and the doctor, I am the only person who knows.

We are having a brand new Butterfield.

For Christmas.

# Chapter 17

'Nothing grows in our garden!' complains V who's been poking about in the earth under her red wool. She plonks herself grumpily down next to me on the grass where I'm reading a book. 'When will my seeds turn into plants?'

It's a very hot Sunday and we are all out in the garden except for Mum who's having a lie-down and Dad who's painting her.

Obviously, I don't mean actually

putting paint on her like a fence or a wall. I mean doing a painting of her while she's resting.

We've got paintings Dad's done of us all over the house. In every one we are asleep. He says no one will sit still long enough when we're awake.

Normally I'd be worried about Mum having a lie-down in the middle of the day but today I'm not because I know the reason why.

Stan sits down opposite us. Immediately, Anika plants her bottom firmly on his lap  and Stan disappears from sight.

'It'll tell you on the packet.' Dontie,

who is sifting through the box of seeds, tosses the one with the picture of spinach on it to V.

She studies it for a while and then chucks it down on the ground.

'What does it say?'

'Nothing. It's stupid.'

V hates reading. It's funny because V is really clever and knows a lot about everything. Mum tries to encourage her but my sister gets really cross and won't do it.

At school she spends a lot of time sitting outside Mrs McFarlane's office. Mrs McFarlane is the Headteacher. Sometimes she calls Mum up to school for a chat and then V tries harder for a while.

And then she stops trying and gets in trouble again.

I include V on my Worry List. She's number 5.

Today, these are my worries.

1 Why aren't the seeds growing?

2 Will we need to grow more now we are having a new baby?

3 Why must we especially not tell Grandma that we're having a new baby?

4 Who will Lucinda live with if her parents get divorced? ( I don't know if Lucinda thinks about this, but I do. A lot.)

5 Why won't V read?

I don't like to bother Mum with these worries at the moment so I shove them behind the Worry Door. Firmly. Then I notice that even though it's baking hot today, like the inside of an oven, it's gone very dark. Big black clouds are blocking out the sun.

Suddenly there's a deep rumble of thunder followed by a huge crack of lightning that makes us all jump, even Dontie. Jellico leaps up and barks as big splashes of rain fall out of the sky.

'Quick!' I say, plucking Anika from Stan's lap, and we run indoors to watch the storm from the window.

'There's nothing to do!' moans V as the thunder and lightning subside but the rain still beats down on the sculptures outside.

'Yes there is!' says Mum as she comes

downstairs. 'There's always things to do on a rainy day.'

'Like what?' says V moodily.

'We could make posters and prices for a stall. Then, if there's any veg left over, we could sell it!'

So Dad fetches paper and felt tips and scissors and we spend the afternoon around the kitchen table making posters and neat little price tags for our veggies.

Dad draws us the outlines of the vegetables and I write their names alongside in my best handwriting. Then Stan and V carefully colour them in while Anika has a sleep.

'Well done, you two,' says Mum and they both look pleased.

But I can't help noticing that Stan's colouring-in is much neater than V's because he keeps inside the lines.

Then V helps Mum to work out the price in kilos for each vegetable because she can do it in her head. (See what I mean? She's really clever!) Dontie writes them in next to their names.

'Good work all of you!' says Dad when we've finished. 'Now all we need is some vegetables to sell.'

'The sun's out!' says V and she dashes outside. Suddenly there's a screech.

'What's happened?' yells Mum and we all run outside. V is bending over the veggie plot.

'Look!' she shouts and points at the ground.

Tiny green shoots are poking through the soil.

## Chapter 18

Before long plants are sprouting up all over the vegetable plot.

Actually, that's not quite true.

The sprouts are *not* sprouting.

That's because Uncle Vez says they take an extra long time and so we won't be able to eat them this summer.

V says she won't eat them this summer or winter or any other time come to that.

'I'm allergic to sprouts,' she says.

'And I'm allergic to naughty little girls

who won't eat up their greens,' says Grandma.

Uncle Vesuvius comes round every night to help us. He shows us how to weed carefully between the plants so they can breathe and how to water them so they don't dry out.

We all look after our own plants.

V is worried because there is no sign of her spinach even though she inspects her patch every five minutes. But at last it appears and then it grows super-fast.

Stanika and I have to water our beans and peas loads because they get so thirsty.

Dontie's rocket and lettuce come on quickly and he doesn't even do anything.

'Mine's the best!' says V.

'It's not a competition!' says Mum.

But V thinks it is.

'Looks like you're going to have a bumper crop here,' says Uncle Vez and he puffs on his biro with satisfaction.

'Well done!' Grandma looks surprised.

Mum looks proud. 'They've all worked really hard.'

'Dontie hasn't!' points out V.

But then, all of a sudden, things go wrong.

Stanika's carrots and peas and sweetcorn and beetroots start looking straggly and sorry for themselves.

And V's plants are disappearing fast.

Uncle Vez can't understand it. He pulls his hat off and scratches his head.

'Have you been looking after these properly, Stan?'

Stanika stare at Uncle Vez reproachfully.

I don't like to say this, Uncle Vez, but

that is a very silly question. Stan always looks after everything properly.

'What about you, V?' he asks.

'Of course I have!' V looks indignant. 'I've been weeding and watering them, just like you said!'

'Don't worry,' says Mum. 'We'll find out what's going wrong.'

Tonight, Mum and Uncle Vez watch very carefully as we see to our vegetables.

They watch as I weed and water my beans and squash.

'Splendid,' says Uncle Vez.

They watch as Stanika weed and water their carrots, peas, sweetcorn and beetroot.

'Excellent!' says Mum.

Then they watch as Stanika dig them back up again carefully to see how they're doing.

'Ah!' says Uncle V. 'That explains it. Don't dig them up Stanika.'

They watch as V waters her pumpkin and spinach.

'That's the way!' says Uncle Vez.

Then they watch as she weeds out half her plants.

'Ah!' says Mum. 'Weed out the weeds, not your plants, V.'

'But they all look the same,' says V, looking puzzled.

Dontie laughs. 'Can't you tell the difference between plants and weeds?'

'Yes!' says V and she stamps her foot.

'Never mind,' says Uncle Vez. 'They could do with thinning out a bit. Otherwise they'll get all thin and spindly.'

'I knew that!' says V, but she doesn't fool anybody.

'Do what I do,' says Dontie, looking smug. 'Leave them to get on with it themselves.'

We turn and stare at his lettuces, growing obediently in nice straight rows with solid little hearts and pretty, curled leaves.

Dontie picks up his football and starts to play keepy-uppy.

I don't think it's fair how some people are good at everything without even trying.

Jellico barks and bounds after him, trying to get the ball.

Dontie gives it a massive kick, high up into the sky.

Jellico leaps high up into the air after it.

And then Jellico lands back down,

SPLAT!

Right in the middle of the vegetable patch.

Right on top of Dontie's neat row of lettuces.

# Chapter 19

After that the veggies come on really well. Even Dontie's lettuces.

That's because lots of people are helping.

Lucinda brings her mum around and she says we're doing splendidly and gives us some radish and broccoli and turnip seeds to sow for winter.

'How are things?' asks Mum and Lucinda's mum sighs. Then they disappear inside the house for a cup of coffee.

Uncle Vez says we'll need a bigger veggie patch now and digs up the soil between Superman and the turtles.

Then he finds some more horse poo to spread on it and stinks the house out again and we all complain.

But Grandma says, 'Well done! Just what it needs.'

Donte makes an observation. 'Grandma is Uncle Vesuvius's VBF now.'

'What's a VBF?' asks V.

'Very best friend,' I explain and V says, 'I knew that!'

Grandma comes by every evening to give Uncle Vez a hand. Granddad comes too but he sits outside on the bench and reads his paper because he's got a bad back.

We have our tea in peace now because

Grandma's busy in the garden. Through the open window we can hear her and Uncle Vez chatting away nineteen to the dozen about *feeding* and *mulching* and *aphids* and *greenfly.*

Dontie makes up a song about them. It goes like this to the tune of 'Pop goes the weasel.'

Half a pound of veggie seed,
Half a pound of mulch goo.
Mix it up with lots of feed,
Grow it all in horse poo.

Half a pound of snails and slugs,
Half a pound of grubs, too.
Caterpillars, cabbage bugs,
Drown them all in horse poo.

Half a pound of household waste,
Makes you sneeze, atishoo!
Gives our veg a lovely taste,
Top it up with horse poo.

Half a pound of sprouts and peas,
Come and eat our nice stew.
Full of carrots, spuds and swede
Grown by us in horse poo.

'Don't let Grandma hear you!' says Mum laughing.

But, guess what!

When Grandma hears us singing it, she laughs too.

And the next evening, while we're having our tea, we can hear Grandma and Uncle Vez singing our song as they hoe up and down between the rows.

'I don't believe it!' says Mum.

So Dad does a quick sketch of them to prove it.

# Chapter 20

Dad says it's time to sell our produce before school breaks up and we go on holiday. He puts a trestle table outside our front garden with Mum's kitchen scales on it.

On the table we place:

- 3 bunches of tiny, twisted carrots
- 12 pods of peas
- 6 little beetroots
- 5 broad bean pods

* 1 small squash
* 2 spinach plants
* and a pile of loose leaves.

No sweetcorn because they won't be ready 'til later in the summer.

No pumpkin because they won't be ready 'til Hallowe'en.

No sprouts because they won't be ready 'til Christmas.

Even when we spread them out, it doesn't look much.

Then Dontie comes out carrying 12 lettuces and a big bundle of rocket.

'Here you are,' he says and dumps them on the table. 'I'm off to play football.'

So V, Stanika, Jellico and I sit down behind the trestle table and wait.

12 people walk past and buy a lettuce.

4 people walk past and buy some rocket.

2 people buy the spinach plants.

3 people buy the loose leaves.

Half an hour later, Lucinda and her mum walk past.

They buy a bunch of carrots, 3 beetroots and the squash.

I am a bit surprised by this because I know Lucinda's mum has got a row of

BUY YOUR
VEG HERE

carrots and a row of beetroot of her own in her organic vegetable garden.

We sit there a bit longer.

One hour and ten minutes longer to be precise.

Lots more people walk past but no one buys the rest of the carrots or beetroot, the peas or the beans.

PRICES

PEAS £1
per kilo

Then Grandma and Granddad come along. Grandma has her net shopping bag with her.

'Dear me!' she says. 'Is that all that's left? You've done well.' She takes out her purse.

'Would you like to buy something, Grandma?' asks Stanley.

'Yes please. I'd like 2 bunches of carrots, 3 beetroot, and I'll take the peas and those broad beans please.'

'That's 30p for the bunch of carrots, 10p each for the beetroot and I'll weigh the rest for you,' says V obligingly.

She plonks the peas on the scale, does some calculations in her head and mutters to herself. Then she says, '25p'.

She puts the beans on the scale, does some more calculations and muttering and then says, '9p'.

Then she rolls up her eyes and says, '30p, 30p, 25p, 9p ... that's 94 pence altogether, please. Would you like a bag?'

Grandma's eyes are wide with astonishment.

'How did you do that?' she asks.

'I don't know. I just did it in my head. It's easy,' says V, dusting her hands. 'Right, that's it. We're sold out.'

'All gone,' agrees Anika.

Five pairs of eyes turn towards my little sister. No, six pairs of eyes. Even Jellico is staring at her in surprise.

'Anika spoke,' says Stanley proudly.

# Chapter 21

We count up the money we've made. It comes to £8.31 altogether. I arrange it nicely in neat stacks of different coins.

'How much did my lettuce and rocket make?' asks Dontie when he comes home.

'£4.80,' says V, quick as a flash.

'Not bad,' he says and stretches out his hand for the money.

My arms encircle the small towers of coins, protecting it like a moat around a castle.

'I'm giving mine to Mum.'

Everyone's faces change.

Stanika's faces brighten.

V's face darkens.

Dontie's jaw drops like a lift shaft. 'How much did you make, Mattie?' he asks.

'34 pence.' V answers for me. 'I made £1.00 on *my* spinach.'

Then she adds, so quickly it's like she's afraid she might change her mind if she stops for breath, 'I'm going to give it to Mum too.'

'Right,' says Dontie. 'Right,' he says again and digs his hands deep into his pockets. Then he slams his football hard into the wall. Twice.

'OK,' he says finally, 'I'm giving mine too.' His voice sounds funny. Squeaky.

'And me,' says Stan.

'And me,' echoes Anika.

I scoop it all back into the jar and we troop into the house.

Inside, Grandma has made us soup for lunch out of the vegetables she bought from our stall. We sit around the kitchen table.

'Something smells good,' says a voice and Uncle Vez walks in.

'Plenty more where that came from,' says Grandma and fills a bowl up for him.

He sits down to take his first slurp. 'Delicious!' he says.

'They grew all of this!' says Grandma.

Uncle Vez takes another mouthful. 'Nature's a wonderful thing,' he says.

'How did you get on?' asks another voice.

Lucinda and her mum are standing at the door.

'Sold out!' says Grandma. 'Come and join us for lunch.'

'My dad's got a new job,' says Lucinda as she sits down next to me.

'Starts on Monday,' adds her mum, looking pink and pleased.

Mum gives her a hug.

Grandma joins us at the table.

'You all did really well,' she announces. 'Grew these vegetables from scratch, you did.'

'It was fun!' says V.

'As for you!' Grandma points her spoon at her and V looks alarmed. 'Bright as a button, you are. You could work out those prices like nobody's business.'

V blushes with pride.

Grandma leans over and whispers in her ear for us not to hear. But I did.

She said, 'Next thing we'll do, we'll get that reading sorted out for you, once and for all.'

And guess what? V doesn't pull a face. Instead she looks up at Grandma and nods.

Do you know something?

V and Grandma don't just look alike when they're scowling.

They look alike when they're smiling too.

# Chapter 22

I push the jar with the money in across the table towards Mum.

'This is for you,' I say.

'What a good girl!' says Grandma.

'It's from all of us.'

'Really?' Grandma looks at V and Dontie in surprise. V nods proudly and Dontie shrugs.

'You're all good kids,' says Granddad fondly. 'Aren't they Marjorie?'

'Indeed they are,' says Grandma. 'You should be proud of them, you two.'

'We are,' say Mum and Dad.

I look around the table and my tummy glows. Everyone is happy today. And for once in my life, I have no worries.

'But I can't take this money,' says Mum. 'You keep it.'

'OK.' Dontie and leans forward to take the jam jar.

'No!' I say. 'It's for the new—!'

And just in time I stop.

'New what?' says Grandma, who doesn't miss a trick.

Mum frowns.

**BIG WORRY!** I'm not supposed to say anything.

Everyone is waiting for my answer.

'New hat?' prompts Uncle Vez.

'New moon?' laughs Dontie.

'New start?' asks Lucinda.

'New dress?' guesses V.

'New age?' suggests Lucinda's mum.

'New tooth?' says Stanley hopefully because he's waiting for one and everyone laughs.

Everyone except Grandma.

'New what?' she repeats.

Mum looks at Dad.

Dad looks at Mum.

Mum nods.

Dad clears his throat.

'New baby,' he says.

The whole table falls silent.

Uncle V takes a final slurp of soup and leans back in his chair. He puts his thumbs in the braces that keep his trousers up and belches comfortably.

'Perfect,' he sighs. 'Like I said, nature's a wonderful thing.'

THE END

# My Funny Family –
# What Happens Next

## My Funny Family On Holiday

It's the summer holidays and the Butterfield family is going away to Cornwall. As usual, Mattie has plenty to worry about. What if she loses the luggage she's been put in charge of? What if someone falls over a cliff? And worst of all ... what if they've forgotten someone?

## My Funny Family Gets Bigger

It's the new school term and, as the baby in Mum's tummy gets bigger and bigger, the family begins to plan for Christmas – making lists and wrapping presents. But could an unexpected Christmas gift be just around the corner?

Before writing her first novel, Chris Higgins taught English and Drama for many years in secondary schools and also worked at the Minack, the open-air theatre on the cliffs near Lands End. She now writes full time and is the author of ten books for children and teenagers.

Chris is married with four daughters. She loves to travel and has lived and worked in Australia as well as hitchhiking to Istanbul and across the Serengeti Plain. Born and brought up in South Wales, she now lives in the far west of Cornwall with her husband.